S0-AZF-777

A TASTE OF
INDIA

Roz Denny

RSVP
RAINTREE
STECK-VAUGHN
P U B L I S H E R S
The Steck-Vaughn Company

Austin, Texas

Titles in this series

A TASTE OF

Britain	Italy
China	Japan
France	Mexico
India	West Africa

Cover *The beautiful Taj Mahal palace is one of India's most famous landmarks.*

Frontispiece *Indians like snacks. These are made from rice, potatoes, and chickpeas.*

UK version copyright © 1994 Wayland (Publishers) Ltd.

U.S. version copyright © 1994 Thomson Learning

This edition published by Raintree Steck-Vaughn, an imprint of Steck-Vaughn Company

Library of Congress Cataloging-in-Publication Data
Denny, Roz.
A taste of India / Roz Denny.
p.   cm. —(Food around the world)
Includes bibliographical references and index.
ISBN 0-8172-4855-2
1. Cookery, India—Juvenile literature. 2. Food habits—India—Juvenile literature.
[1. Cookery, India. 2. Food habits—India. 3. India—Social life and customs.]
I. Title. II. Series.
TX724.5.I4D39   1994
641.5954—dc20   93-37197

Printed in Italy. Bound in the United States.
2 3 4 5 6 7 8 9 0 02 01 00 99 98

Contents

India in the world today

India is an important country in the world today. Through its people and culture, its influence has reached many other parts of the world.

India is very densely populated. It is one-third the size of the United States, yet it has about three times the population – more than 850 million. Also, about 17 million more Indians live in other parts of the world, including Britain, the Middle East, Africa, and North America.

India is a very crowded country – and a very colorful one.

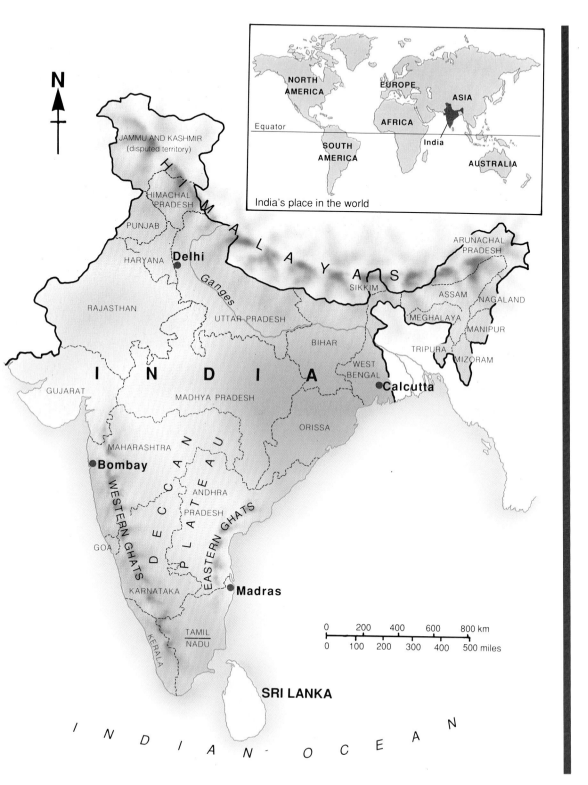

N

JAMMU AND KASHMIR
(disputed territory)

H I M A L A Y A S

HIMACHAL
PRADESH

PUNJAB

HARYANA · Delhi

Ganges

RAJASTHAN

ARUNACHAL
PRADESH

SIKKIM

ASSAM

NAGALAND

UTTAR PRADESH

MEGHALAYA

MANIPUR

BIHAR

TRIPURA

MIZORAM

WEST
BENGAL

I N D I A · Calcutta

GUJARAT

MADHYA PRADESH

ORISSA

MAHARASHTRA

D E C C A N

· Bombay

ANDHRA

PRADESH

WESTERN GHATS

P L A T E A U

GOA

EASTERN GHATS

KARNATAKA

· Madras

TAMIL
NADU

KERALA

SRI LANKA

I N D I A N   O C E A N

NORTH
AMERICA

EUROPE

ASIA

AFRICA

Equator

India

SOUTH
AMERICA

AUSTRALIA

India's place in the world

| 0 | 200 | 400 | 600 | 800 km |
| 0 | 100 | 200 | 300 | 400 | 500 miles |

5

A taste of India

In India there are:
- 25 states and seven territories
- 16 main languages (including English)
- 6 main religious groups (including Hindus, Muslims, Christians, and Sikhs)

With so many different people, no wonder the food of India is so varied and delicious.

Indians are extremely proud of their culture. Although many now live according to Western ways, Indians value their history and pass on their traditions to their children.

The land

Geographers call India a subcontinent because it is so large. It covers an area of more than one million square miles. In fact it is almost big enough to be a continent in itself.

India is a long, pointed land mass, or peninsula, sticking out from the rest of southern Asia. It is bordered to the east and west by seas, and to the north by the largest mountain range in the world – the Himalayas. It has every type of landscape.

A Himalayan landscape in northern India.

In the north are snowy mountains. South of the mountains are thickly wooded foothills and fertile valleys. These in turn give way to a vast, flat plain, containing one of India's great rivers, the Ganges. This plain is the center of Indian culture. Today it is a densely populated area with many big cities, including Delhi, India's capital, and Calcutta.

Southern India juts out into the Indian Ocean. In the center is a high, flat land area called the Deccan Plateau, with a mountain range on either side – the Eastern and Western Ghats. All around are coastal plains. Two other big cities are in southern India – Bombay and Madras. (The large island of Sri Lanka, off the tip of India, is a separate country.)

Above *South of the Himalayas are foothills and green valleys.*
Below *The Thar Desert is very dry. Camels are used because they need very little water.*

Climate

Generally speaking, India is a very hot country. It includes some of the hottest places in the world, with temperatures of up to 100° F. In the north, the climate is temperate, with cold winters, warm summers, and a high rainfall.

On the vast northern plain, the summers are very hot and the winters cold. For much of the year there is very little rain and occasionally there are even dust storms.

Above *Palm trees grow in the tropical coastal areas of southern India.*
Below *The monsoon brings heavy rain.*

The Deccan Plateau is dry too, but the coastal plains around it have a lot of rain. In these parts, tropical plants grow.

There are three seasons in India: cool and dry, hot and dry, and very rainy. This last season is the time of the monsoon winds, which last from June to September. Heavy monsoon rains bring welcome relief from the great heat, plus much-needed water for crops. But the monsoon can also bring flooding and storms called typhoons, which can cause havoc and kill many people. In some years, the monsoon brings too little rain, and crops die.

The history of Indian food

In India, many dishes and recipes date from ancient times. Over 4,000 years ago, one of the world's great ancient civilizations grew up around the Indus River, to the northwest of India. These ancient people learned to control the river's water with dams and canals. They built towns and temples and started to grow crops. Later, various armies of warriors invaded and took control.

One group of these invaders, the Aryans, settled down and continued to develop civilization. They grew crops, such as wheat, barley, and rice. They also introduced a language called Sanskrit, which became the language of the Hindu religion.

In about A.D. 1000 yet another wave of warriors invaded from the northwest. They brought a new religion, the Muslim religion of Islam. The descendants of these invaders were known as Moguls. They formed an important empire that brought great culture to India. They encouraged art, literature, and music.

Above *This carving, found near the Indus River, is about 4,000 years old.*
Below *A picture of the great Mogul emperor, Akbar.*

The beautiful Taj Mahal was built in the seventeenth century by a Mogul emperor in memory of his wife, after her death.

The Moguls also developed delicious recipes and some of India's most famous dishes date from this time.

Food and religion

Millions of Indians are vegetarians because it is against their religion to eat meat. They have delicious ways of cooking lentils, dairy products, vegetables, breads, and rice. In some religions even tomatoes, onions, and root vegetables such as carrots are not permitted.

Over three-quarters of Indians are Hindus. Most Hindus are vegetarians and all Hindus believe cows are sacred animals. So Hindus do not eat beef at all, although foods can be made from cows' milk, including yogurt, cheese, and a clarified butter called *ghee*.

A tenth of Indians are Muslims, who are not allowed to eat pork. Most of the meat dishes in India are made from lamb and chicken.

Foods from the Americas

Following Columbus' voyages to the New World (between 1492 and 1504), the hot chili pepper, which is native to the Americas, was introduced to Europe. From there, it spread quickly to India. Up until then, although Indians had used aromatic spices, their food had not been spicy hot as much of it is now. Other foods from the Americas, such as tomatoes and potatoes, also became popular with Indian cooks.

Hot chili peppers left to dry.

The British in India

In the seventeenth century the British set up a trading company in India, known as the East India Company. Eventually, this led to British control of all of India.

The system of British rule in India became known as the British Raj. Many popular British dishes today are based on Indian recipes, such as chutney, curry, kedgeree, and rice pudding. Now, the joy of Indian food has spread around the world, and many restaurants serve delicious, spiced dishes.

Kedgeree is a British dish of rice, fish, egg, and, usually, curry powder.

11

Food from the regions

The dishes that India is most famous for – the ones now eaten in restaurants around the world – come from different regions of the country. For example, *tikka* and *tandoori* were developed by warriors from Rajasthan in northwest India. To make *tikka* they grilled their pieces of meat on skewers (or maybe the warriors used their swords). First, the meat was marinated with spices and oil or yogurt. Larger pieces of meat were roasted in a special clay-lined oven called a *tandoor* – hence *tandoori* meat.

A tandoor *is an oven lined with clay. This one is being used to cook* naan, *a type of bread.*

Next to Rajasthan is the state of Gujarat, which is famous for its vegetarian dishes. Gujaratis use many types of vegetables, legumes such as lentils, breads, rice, yogurt, eggs, and a kind of cottage cheese called *paneer.*

In southern India, rice is very popular. Fish is also often eaten around the coast. Many meat dishes come from the Muslim state of Andhra Pradesh: there is *korma* (a creamy, mildly spiced meat dish) and *biriyani*, a rich dish of rice and meat often cooked at festivals.

One of India's hottest dishes, *vindaloo*, contains plenty of fiery chilies and is often cooked with pork. It comes from the Christian area of Goa, on the west coast, where the Portuguese settled many centuries ago.

Locally caught fish is used in many dishes in southern India.

Farming and crops

Farmers all over India use cattle to pull their plows. In the background of this picture is a field of sugarcane.

Irrigation (watering the land) is important in dry areas. This village uses water from a well to irrigate the land and produce more crops.

Nearly three-fourths of Indians are farmers and most of them own very small areas of land – barely enough to grow food for one family. Many villages are still without good drainage, electricity, or modern tools. Unless farming methods are improved, there will not be enough food to feed India's growing population. In some villages, the people have joined together to form cooperatives, or groups that help each other to farm the land. In these places life has improved. However, poverty is still a great problem in India and disease and hunger remain.

A family of Indian peasant farmers all work together. The mother gets up first to clean the house and prepare a simple breakfast. Then the father goes into the fields by 6 a.m. and works in the great heat with only a short break at lunchtime. In busy periods, children also help in the fields after school.

The main food crops in India are rice, wheat, sugarcane, and legumes. Tea is also grown and is exported to other countries.

Rice

India is the world's second largest grower of rice, after China. The average Indian eats about 7 ounces of rice a day – that is about 160 pounds a year! In the United States the average is 20.5 pounds a year.

This girl is helping her mother to plant crops. Many children help in the fields after school.

Rice seedlings are planted in paddies.

A taste of India

Growing rice involves several stages. The seeds are sown and grown into seedlings. Then, the rice seedlings are replanted by hand in fields that have been flooded with water. This fertilizes and waters the rice, and stops attacks on it by insects.

There are many varieties of rice grown in India. The most popular are long-grain rices. A very high-quality rice, *basmati*, is grown in the foothills of the Himalayas and is expensive because it grows quite slowly. *Basmati* smells delicious: the name means "the fragrant one" in Hindi.

Cook your own perfect rice

Ingredients
Serves 4

1 cup *basmati* rice
2 tablespoons vegetable oil
1 teaspoon salt
$2^1/_2$ cups water

Cooked basmati *rice.*

Equipment

strainer
large saucepan
wooden spoon
fork

1   Rinse the rice in a sieve under cold running water. Drain well.

2   Heat the oil in the saucepan and fry the rice, stirring with a wooden spoon, for about a minute.

3   Pour in the water, add the salt, and bring to a boil. Cover with a lid, then lower the heat to a gentle simmer. Cook for 12 minutes. No peeking, or you will let out the steam!

4   Remove the pan from the heat with the lid still on. Leave for 5 minutes, then uncover and stir with a fork.

Always be careful with boiling liquid. Ask an adult to help you.

A taste of India

Women pick tea leaves by hand.

Tea

The northern hilly regions of Assam and Darjeeling have some of the highest rainfall in the world, sometimes up to 75 inches a year. This is ideal for growing tea. Tea, called *chay* in India, is drunk all over the country, and great amounts are exported around the world.

Tea is grown on plantations. The tea leaves are picked by hand by women. Only the very tips are picked. It is extremely hard work.

Much of the tea from Assam ends up in our tea bags. Darjeeling tea is of higher quality and most of it is still sold as leaves to be brewed in the traditional way using a pot and strainer.

Chay (Indian tea) is made by boiling water, milk, sugar, and spices with tea leaves, then straining it into small cups.

Indian tea is not like the tea drunk in Western countries. It is boiled in a pan.

Cooking and eating in India

Some Indians have kitchens similar to those in the West. But many millions of people cook over one burner, often outdoors. The fuel might be wood, charcoal, or cow dung mixed with straw and baked in the sun until it is hard. Some people have a gas burner. Cooking is usually done in batches. The food is reheated quickly before serving if necessary.

An outdoor kitchen in northern India. Many people cook outdoors.

Idlis *(steamed rice cakes) are eaten for breakfast.*

A meal may consist of rice, vegetables, and meat or lentils.

Mealtimes

Indians like to eat three good hot meals a day. Breakfast is often reheated spiced rice and breads left over from the day before. In southern India, breakfast might consist of steamed rice cakes, called *idlis*, or rice pancakes called *dosa*. Sometimes *chapatis* (flat breads) are cut into pieces, fried in spicy oil, and mixed with yogurt, garlic, and spices.

Lunch is a full meal with rice, breads, cooked vegetables, *raitas* (chopped or grated raw vegetables, such as cucumber or beets, with yogurt), and a main dish of lentils or meat.

People who work away from home will have their lunches brought to them in "tiffin" boxes. These are round metal food containers, stacked on top of each other, with carrying handles. At about 11 a.m. each day, special "tiffin-carriers" called *dabba wallahs* collect tiffin boxes from people's houses and take them to offices or schools so that members of the family can eat their lunches.

The evening meal is yet another delicious home-cooked meal. All meals in India are served with lots of pickles, relishes, and *raitas.*

A man carrying a tiffin box at lunchtime.

Snack food

The railroads of India are world famous. Many people travel long distances on them. At every station, and inside the trains too, food and drink vendors offer delicious snacks and sweet treats. When the train stops at a station, food vendors knock on the windows and offer travelers snacks and *chay* in small cups.

Indians also enjoy little snacks during the day. Most popular are *papadums,* thin rounds of bread made with lentil flour and dried in the sun. They get crisp when grilled on an open fire.

A taste of India

Samosas
Other popular snacks include *samosas*. These are little triangles of fried, wafer-thin pastry wrapped around spicy fillings of vegetables, legumes, or meat.

Samosas can be bought from food stalls.

Eating in India – using one hand and a chapati. *You may hold the* chapati *in your left hand, but you must use your right to scoop the food and eat it.*

How to eat Indian-style
While many city people might eat with knives and forks, most Indians still use their fingers because they like to feel the lovely texture of their food. There is quite a knack to doing it neatly. Here are some tips:
- Always use your right hand. It is bad manners to eat with your left hand. Wash both hands very well before you begin.
- Tear off a piece of *chapati*, about the size of half a small saucer.
- Fold it to form a scoop, shovel up the food from a plate, then pop it into your mouth.
- Remember, you must use only one hand to tear, fold, and scoop, so keep practicing.

Spices and curries

The word "curry" is an English term used to describe the spicy stews eaten by Indians. The word is thought to come from the south of India, where a people called the Tamils live. The Tamils call their spicy sauces "*kari.*" The word "curry" is not used by Indians.

Spices are so important in all Indian food that is hard to imagine a meal without them. They give a delicious, aromatic flavor to even the simplest of foods. Children in India are not fussy eaters and enjoy the lightly spiced sauces; fragrant, fresh, flat breads; rice; and vegetables India is well known for. Very young children do not eat highly spiced foods, but most Indians grow up with spices.

Bags of spices for sale at a city market.

A taste of India

A basket of crocus flowers that will be used to make saffron.

Chili peppers give Indian food its hot spiciness.

The main spices used in India

Cumin Small, long, thin seeds, which are ground up to make a powder.

Coriander Small, pale-brown, round, dried berries. The leaves, too, are used. The leaves are similar to parsley, but hot.

Asafetida A strong, bitter powder used to bring out the flavor of food.

Fenugreek Small, pale-yellow, square-shaped seeds.

Ginger A hot-tasting root. It is used fresh (grated or chopped) or dried (as a powder).

Cinnamon Long, thin pieces of rolled tree bark.

Cloves Dried, unopened flower buds from the clove tree. They have a very strong taste if you bite them.

Cardamom Pods with green outer casings and small, aromatic black seeds inside.

Chilies Fresh green or dried red chilies are spicy hot and should be used carefully because they can cause stinging. Wash your hands after cutting them, or use rubber gloves. Be careful not to rub your eyes.

Fennel Small seeds with an anise or licorice flavor.

Garam masala A mixture of spices all ground together. Cooks often make their own blend.

Turmeric When fresh, this is a root like ginger, but it is often sold dried and ground into a powder. It turns food bright yellow.

Mustard seeds and **poppy seeds** Small, black, round seeds. They pop when heated in a pan.

Saffron Probably the world's most expensive spice, saffron is used only for special dishes. It comes from a particular crocus and turns food reddish yellow.

Cooking with spices

Most Indians buy spices whole and grind them to a powder using a pestle and mortar. The spices are stored in small, round cans contained in another, larger, round can.

Spices are always best if they are lightly heated before they are ground. This brings out the fullest flavor. When they are used, the ground spices are fried briefly in hot oil before the rest of the cooking to bring out more flavor.

This woman is sorting coriander seeds.

Three forms of cinnamon: (from top) the bark; rolled into sticks; ground into powder.

Other everyday foods

Indian breads

Bread is very important in India. It is eaten at every meal and there is a great variety of types. Most of it is unleavened. This means it is not made to rise with yeast, like the sliced bread used in the West for sandwiches or toast. Instead it remains flat.

The most common breads are *chapatis* and the slightly richer *parathas*, which can be stuffed with vegetables and minced meat. Small balls of dough are rolled out into thin rounds, then cooked

Making chapatis. *Small balls of dough are rolled out and cooked on a hot metal plate.*

quickly on heavy, metal hot plates called *tavas*. It takes a long time to learn to roll the dough with one hand while you flip the cooked bread with the other – even more difficult when you have to squat by an open wood or charcoal fire, fanning it occasionally to keep the flames going.

Other breads, called *purees*, are small and puffy. They are deep-fried in hot oil in a pan that looks like a Chinese wok. Little rounds of dough are slipped carefully into the oil; they puff up almost instantly.

Naan breads are made from dough leavened with yeast. This causes them to rise a little.

Puffy purees *are another kind of unleavened bread.*

A taste of India

Vegetables for sale at a market.

A dish of spicy okra.

Vegetables

Because India has so many vegetarians, there are many wonderful vegetables and recipes for cooking them. Here are some popular vegetables.

Eggplant Long and thick with shiny purple skins. When cooked, they get soft and creamy.

Spinach Green, leafy, and very nutritious. In India it is often fried with spices.

Okra (sometimes known as ladies' fingers) Long and green with small seeds inside. Okra is often used in stews.

Potatoes Very popular, especially in vegetarian dishes.

Cauliflower Again, very popular and often cooked with whole spices.

Indians also use other vegetables eaten all over the world, such as peas, peppers, beans, cabbage, tomatoes, carrots, and mushrooms. Almost all vegetables are cooked in delicious ways, using spices, onions, garlic, ginger, and coconut cream.

Pulses

Pulses, or legumes, are the seeds of pod-bearing plants. They are very healthy foods because they contain a lot of proteins. Protein helps us to grow and keep up our strength. Meat is an excellent source of protein, but because most Indians are vegetarians they have to get their protein from vegetable foods such as pulses.

Neat piles of pulses on sale at a street stall. There are many different shapes and colors of pulses.

A taste of India

Lentils are cooked with spices to make a kind of runny stew.

Lentils and split peas (both of which Indians call *dhal*) and dried beans are all pulses. When cooked, pulses can either be creamy or firm. Here are some of the most popular ones.

Masoor dhal A type of lentil with a brown skin and orangy-yellow inside.

Green lentils Flat, greeny-brown, disk-shaped lentils.

Chickpeas, red kidney beans, and **aduki beans** Firm beans that hold their shape well when cooked.

Drinks

There are lots of popular drinks in India. In towns and cities you will find many street stalls where you can buy drinks as a quick refreshment. Spiced tea (called *masal chay*) is made by boiling milk, water, and sugar with tea leaves and spices such as cloves, cinnamon, and cardamom.

Lassi is a cool yogurt drink made of yogurt curd mixed with water, salt or sugar, and sometimes mint or mangos.

India grows a lot of sugarcane. When the stalks are crushed, the sweet juice is mixed with fresh lime juice or fresh ginger to make a refreshing drink called *Ghanna* juice.

However, as in the rest of the world, fizzy, sweet, cola-type drinks are also popular in India.

A drink stall in Bombay features fresh fruit juices as well as bottled fizzy drinks.

Sweets and desserts

Indians love sweet foods, which they usually serve at the end of a meal or as snacks. Sweet, thick *purees*, called *halvas*, are very popular. These are made from carrots or semolina, flavored with spices such as cardamom, and have almonds, pistachio nuts, or raisins stirred in.

Traditional Indian sweets: the yellow square (center) is a halva; *the yellow balls are called* ladu *and are eaten at weddings; the rest are sweets made from milk, with nuts or spices added.*

Light, milk puddings, called *kheer*, are made with rice or vermicelli and often flavored with rose water or almonds. Indian ice cream, called *kulfi*, is very rich and comes in flavors such as mango or pistachio.

31

Festival food

Indians love to celebrate, whether it is a wedding or other religious festival. Some celebrations can go on for days, and food plays an important part.

At weddings, rice and rose petals are thrown over the happy couple for good luck. This is where the Western custom of throwing rice and confetti comes from. No matter what the religion of the people involved, an important part of an Indian wedding is the sweet dish served during the meal. Although it is sweet,

These delicious-looking dishes were prepared for a wedding. The food is kept in large pots until the guests are ready to eat.

At the festival of Diwali, Hindus light lamps or candles.

it is actually the main dish and is the middle course. Many different types of sweet foods may be served. Some of the most popular are pastries made from semolina dough fried in hot *ghee* and sweetened with sugar or syrup.

The most important religious festival for Hindus is called *Diwali*, the festival of lights. It is a magical time when streets, homes, and public buildings are all lit up. Friends exchange candy, nuts, and fruits. There are fireworks and fairs. Because *Diwali* is a Hindu festival no meat is served, but all the food is rich, made in special ways, using lots of spices, butter, and nuts. Candy and desserts have wafer-thin layers of real silver leaf placed on top. Even the silver can be eaten.

The most important Muslim festival is *Id,* which marks the end of the month of Ramadan. During Ramadan Muslims over the age of twelve fast, which means they do not eat or drink during daylight hours. Muslims celebrate the festival of *Id* with spicy meat dishes and sweets.

This procession in Bombay is being held to celebrate the Muslim festival of Id.

Kitchidi

Ingredients
Serves 4-6
1 cup long grain rice
1 onion, peeled
1 small green pepper
1 clove garlic, peeled
2 tablespoons butter
1 tablespoon oil
1 teaspoon ground
     turmeric
1 teaspoon ground
     coriander
$1/2$ teaspoon ground
     cumin
1 lb can green lentils,
     drained, or dried
     lentils prepared
     according to the
     directions on the
     package
2 tablespoons fresh
     chopped parsley or
     coriander
salt and black pepper

The British breakfast dish, kedgeree, is supposed to have developed from this Indian recipe. *Kitchidi* is a very healthy and tasty dish.

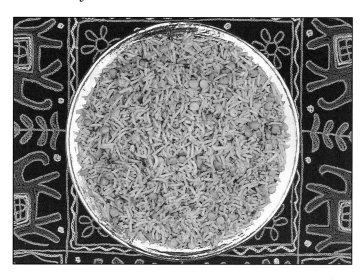

Kitchidi *is a combination of rice and lentils.*

Equipment

1 medium saucepan	can opener
1 large saucepan	garlic press
knife	wooden spoon
chopping board	serving dish

Always be careful with hot oil and boiling liquid. Ask an adult to help you.

1 Boil the rice in 2 cups of water according to the instructions on pages 16-17. Keep it warm.

2 Chop the onion very fine. Cut the pepper in half, remove the seeds and core. Chop the pepper very fine. Crush the garlic in a garlic press.

3 In a large saucepan, melt the butter with the oil and gently fry the onion, pepper, and garlic for about 5 minutes until softened.

4 Stir in the spices and cook for 1 minute. Then add $1^{3/4}$ cups water and the lentils. Bring to a boil, then add a little salt and pepper.

5 Simmer for 10 minutes, stirring once or twice, then mix in the rice. Cook for 3 more minutes. Serve hot, spooned onto a serving dish and sprinkled with fresh chopped parsley or coriander.

Naan

This is a leavened bread, made with yeast.

Naan *breads.*

1 Sift the flour into a big bowl. Add the yeast and salt and stir in the seeds.

2 Mix the yogurt, water, and butter together and stir into the flour with a big wooden spoon.

3 With clean hands, turn the dough out onto a board. Rub the dough hard as if you were scrubbing clothes. This is called kneading and makes the dough nice and smooth. Do this for at least 5 minutes.

4 Put the dough back in the bowl, cover with plastic wrap, and let it rise in a warm part of the kitchen until it has doubled in size. This will take between 2 and 4 hours, depending on the warmth of the room.

Always be careful with hot oil and pans. Ask an adult to help you.

5 Punch the dough so that it collapses. Take it out of the bowl and knead it again for 1 minute. Cut it into 8 equal pieces and roll each into a ball.

6 Sprinkle a little flour on a work surface and roll each ball out to an oval shape (the Indians say "like a teardrop").

7 Heat a griddle or heavy-based frying pan until quite hot, brush it lightly with some oil, and cook each bread for about 3 minutes on each side. Watch to see that it does not burn. Keep the breads warm, wrapped in a clean tea towel, while you make the rest.

Vermicelli pudding

Ingredients
Serves 4-6

$2^{1}/_{2}$ oz. vermicelli pasta
3 tablespoons sugar
5 cardamom pods
2 bay leaves
1 quart milk
2–3 tablespoons
    raisins
2 tablespoons slivered
    almonds
5 oz. can evaporated
    milk
freshly grated nutmeg,
    to taste

Equipment

large saucepan
wooden spoon
can opener
pretty serving bowl

Use very thin spaghetti, called vermicelli, for this quick milk pudding.

Kheer *is an Indian milk pudding made with rice, similar to this vermicelli recipe.*

Always be careful with boiling liquid. Ask an adult to help you.

38

Vermicelli pudding

1 Break up the vermicelli into a large saucepan. Add the sugar.

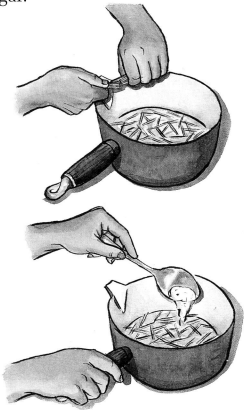

2 Split open the cardamom pods and scrape the small black seeds into the pan. Throw away the outer shells.

3 Add the bay leaves and milk. Bring to a boil, stirring occasionally, then turn the heat down. Do not let it boil over.

4 Simmer the pudding, stirring 2 or 3 times, for 15 minutes.

5 Mix in the raisins, almonds, and evaporated milk. Cool and serve in a pretty glass bowl. If you like, sprinkle the top with some nutmeg.

Tandoori *chicken* drumsticks

Pieces of chicken cooked tandoori-style.

You can use a ready-made Indian *tandoori* paste from a specialty store for this. These pastes are excellent and taste just like homemade ones.

Ingredients
Serves 3-6

6 chicken drumsticks
1 tablespoon *tandoori* paste

²/₃ cup plain natural yogurt
1 teaspoon sea salt
1 lemon
sprigs of fresh coriander, to garnish

Equipment

small bowl
plastic food bag
baking sheet
knife and chopping
    board
serving dish

1   Pull the skin off the chicken and throw it away.

2   Mix the *tandoori* paste with the yogurt and salt in a bowl, then spoon it into the plastic bag.

Always be careful with a hot oven. Ask an adult to help you.

3   Place the chicken pieces in the bag, tie up the top, then squeeze the bag to rub the paste well into the chicken. Refrigerate for 30 minutes while you heat the oven to 350°F.

4   Remove the chicken from the bag (do not worry if it is messy) and place on a baking sheet. Cook in the oven for 25 to 30 minutes.

5   Cut the lemon into 8 wedges. Arrange the chicken on a serving plate and garnish with the lemon and fresh sprigs of coriander. Serve with bread, such as *naan* (recipe on page 36), and *raita* (recipe on page 44).

Lamb and basmati *rice*

This is a rich rice dish, ideal for serving on special occasions such as a party or to celebrate a festival like *Diwali*. You may leave out the saffron since it is expensive, but it *is* delicious. You may also use beef instead of lamb – but not for Hindus.

> Always be careful with hot oil and boiling liquid. Ask an adult to help you.

Ingredients
Serves 4-6

a small piece of fresh ginger root, about ³/₄ inch long
2 cloves garlic, peeled
1 teaspoon ground turmeric
2 tablespoons oil
saffron strands to fill a small teaspoon (optional)
1 lb lean lamb (or beef)
1 large onion, peeled and sliced
1 cup *basmati* rice
2¹/₂ cups water
4 cardamom pods
2 tablespoons fresh, chopped coriander or parsley
juice of 1 small lemon
2 tablespoons butter or *ghee*
salt and pepper
2 tablespoons pistachio nuts or slivered almonds

Equipment

grater
garlic press
large saucepan with lid
wooden spoon
small bowl
knife
chopping board
strainer
cup
lemon squeezer

1 Peel the ginger and grate it. Crush the garlic and, in a small bowl, mix it with the ginger, turmeric, and half the oil to make a paste.

2 If you are using saffron, soak the strands in two tablespoons of hot water and set aside.

3 Heat the remaining oil in the saucepan and fry the meat until well browned, stirring with a wooden spoon. Add the ginger paste and continue frying for 1 minute.

4 Stir in the onion and cook for another 2 minutes.

5 Add the *basmati*, the saffron strands with their soaking water, the $2^1/_2$ cups of water, and the cardamom pods. Cook for a minute and stir again. Add 1 teaspoon of salt, bring to a boil, then turn down the heat to a simmer and cover.

6 Cook for 10 minutes. Remove from the heat and leave for 5 minutes. Do not lift the lid.

7 Uncover, remove the cardamom pods (which will have floated to the top), then stir in the chopped coriander or parsley, lemon juice, and butter or *ghee*. Season with salt and pepper and serve hot, sprinkled with the nuts.

Raita

Raita

Serve this with main course dishes.

1 Grate the cucumber on the biggest holes of the grater and place it in a bowl. Grate in the onion. You do not need much.

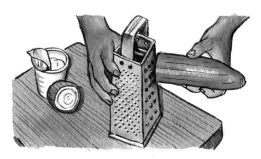

2 Mix in the yogurt, mint, cumin seeds, and some salt and pepper. Spoon into a serving bowl and chill in the refrigerator until serving.

Ingredients
Serves 4

¹/₂ cucumber
¹/₂ small onion, peeled
1 8 oz. carton plain yogurt
2 tablespoons fresh
   chopped mint
¹/₂ teaspoon cumin seeds
salt and ground black
   pepper

Equipment

grater
medium-sized bowl
wooden spoon
serving dish

44

Glossary

Ancient civilization
Societies, or groups of people, that developed thousands of years ago. The ancient civilizations of the world set up highly organized systems of law, farming, building, and the arts. They include the ancient Greeks, ancient Romans, and ancient Egyptians.

Aromatic   Having a strong, pleasant smell.

Chapatis   Round, flat Indian breads. The bread is unleavened, meaning it is not made to rise with yeast.

Charcoal   A fuel made from wood that has been partly burned to make black lumps or sticks.

Chili   A small, hot-tasting green or red pepper. It is often dried and ground to make a powder, and used as a spice.

Culture   The art, history, and traditions that make a society, or group of people, different from any other.

Curd   A firm, creamy substance made from milk. Curd forms when the watery liquid in milk (the whey) separates from it.

Dams   Barriers built across rivers to hold back the water.

Densely populated   Having many people living close together.

Descendents   The children, grandchildren, great-grandchildren, and so on, of people who lived in earlier times.

Dough   A sticky paste made from flour and kneaded until it is very elastic. Bread is made from dough.

Drainage   A system of drains (channels or pipes) used for taking away wastewater and sewage.

Export   To sell food or other goods to countries abroad.

Foothills   The smaller hills that surround a range of high mountains.

Hindi   A language spoken by many people in India. It is one of the country's many official languages.

Marinating Soaking meat or fish in spices with oil, yogurt, or wine to make it flavorful and tender.

Paddies Fields flooded with water for growing rice.

Peninsula A piece of land that sticks out into the sea and is almost completely surrounded by water.

Pestle and mortar A special pounding tool (the pestle) and bowl (the mortar) used for grinding spices and other substances to a powder. In India, these are usually made of stone.

Plantations Large areas of land that have been planted with bushes or trees. On plantations in India, tea, cotton, and rubber trees are grown.

Poverty A serious lack of money that leads to a poor standard of living.

Pulses The seeds of certain pod-bearing plants. Peas, beans, and lentils are all pulses. They are often dried.

Relishes Tasty sauces eaten with other foods to add extra flavor.

Sacred Holy.

Semolina The hard grains left after wheat or other cereals have been ground up to make flour.

Simmer Boil gently.

Spices Strong-tasting substances used to add flavor to food. They are often ground into a powder or paste.

Subcontinent An area of land that is large, but smaller than a continent. The seven continents of the world are Europe, Asia, North America, South America, Africa, Australia, and Antarctica.

Temperate Neither very hot nor very cold.

Traditions The customs passed down by people over the centuries.

Tropical A word that describes the very hot, wet climate of the tropics (the areas just to the north and south of the equator).

Vegetarians People who do not eat meat.

Vermicelli A kind of pasta made in very thin strands.

Yeast A fungus that causes a chemical reaction, called fermentation, when it is added to food. Yeast makes dough rise to make bread.

Further information

Recipe books

Kaur, Sharon. *Food in India.* Vero Beach, FL: Rourke Publications, 1989.

Madavan, Vijay. *Cooking the Indian Way.* Minneapolis: Lerner Pulications, 1985.

Wilkes, Angela. *My First Cookbook.* New York: Alfred A. Knopf, 1989.

Information books

Cumming, David. *India.* Countries of the World. New York: Bookwright Press, 1989.

Das, Prodeepta. *India.* Inside. New York: Franklin Watts, 1990.

Kalman, Bobbie. *India: The Culture.* New York: Crabtree Publishing, 1990.

Nugent, Nicholas. *India.* World in View. Austin: Raintree Steck-Vaughn, 1991.

Acknowledgments

The publishers would like to thank the following for allowing their photographs to be reproduced: Anthony Blake Photo Library 20 top; Bridgeman Art Library 9 both; Cephas 26 (N. Blythe); Chapel Studios *frontispiece*, 11 bottom, 12 (J. Heinrich), 16, 18 top (T. Richardson), 22 top, 25 top, 27, 28 bottom, 30 top, 31, 34, 36, 38, 44; Bruce Coleman Ltd. 6 (G. Cubitt), 8 top (G. Cubitt); Greg Evans International 13 top (G. Evans), 14 top (G. Roy), 15 bottom (R. Van Raders); Eye Ubiquitous 4 (C. Johnson), 7 top , 14 bottom (P. Field), 15 top (P. Bouineau), 18 bottom (P. Smith), 19 (C. Johnson), 22 bottom (D. Cumming), 23, 24 top, 25 bottom (P. Seheult), 29 (D. Cumming), 32, 40 (P. Seheult); Hutchison Library 27, 33 top (L. Taylor), 33 bottom (M. Saunders); Tony Stone Worldwide *cover*, 7 bottom (H. Kavanagh), 10 top (S. and N. Geary), 20 bottom (J. Jackson), 28 top (D. Hanson), 30 bottom (C. Haigh); Wayland Picture Library *cover inset* (A. Blackburn); Zefa 8 bottom, 11 top (Reinhard), 24 bottom.

The map artwork on page 5 was supplied by Peter Bull. The recipe artwork on pages 17 and 35-44 was supplied by Judy Stevens.

The author would like to thank Meena Patak, of Patak Spices, and Mrs. Sandy Samani. Also thanks to Tilda Rice and the Indian High Commission, London.

47

Index